2 MOMMIES + 1 DADDY = ZOE

Written by: Tiffany A. Jackson Harrison

Illustrated by: Saher Nazir

Dedication

This book is dedicated to my daughter,
Zoe Doll Jackson Harrison.

Your birth gave me life.

You are truly our angel from God.

I love you.

Mommy

Zoe is a happy little girl who lives with her two mommies in a house with a huge backyard, with lots of grass and even a treehouse.

Some of Zoe's favorite things are banana-strawberry yogurt, mangoes and her precious bear.

"Bear" is blue and has wings, like an angel. His birthday is very special: July 29, 2012.

Zoe has two mommies.
She calls Tiffany,
"Mommy" and Yvonne,
"Other Mommy."

Zoe also loves her daddy, Ari,
especially when he throws her up
in the air. Zoe is filled with
laughter.

Mommy Yvonne works for a major airline so Zoe can fly all over the world. She loves to visit the aquarium, the zoo and the museum on every trip that they take.

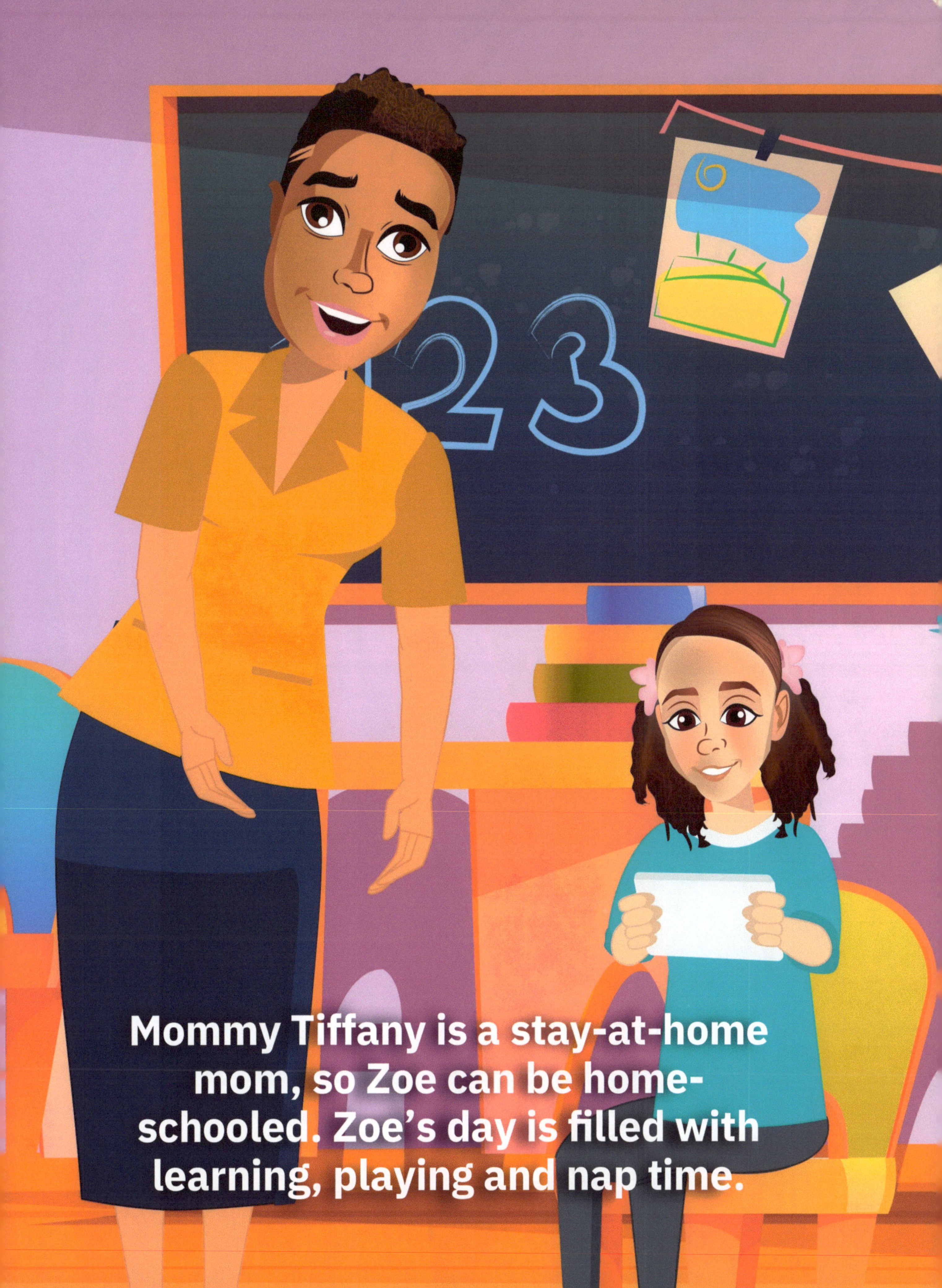

Mommy Tiffany is a stay-at-home mom, so Zoe can be home-schooled. Zoe's day is filled with learning, playing and nap time.

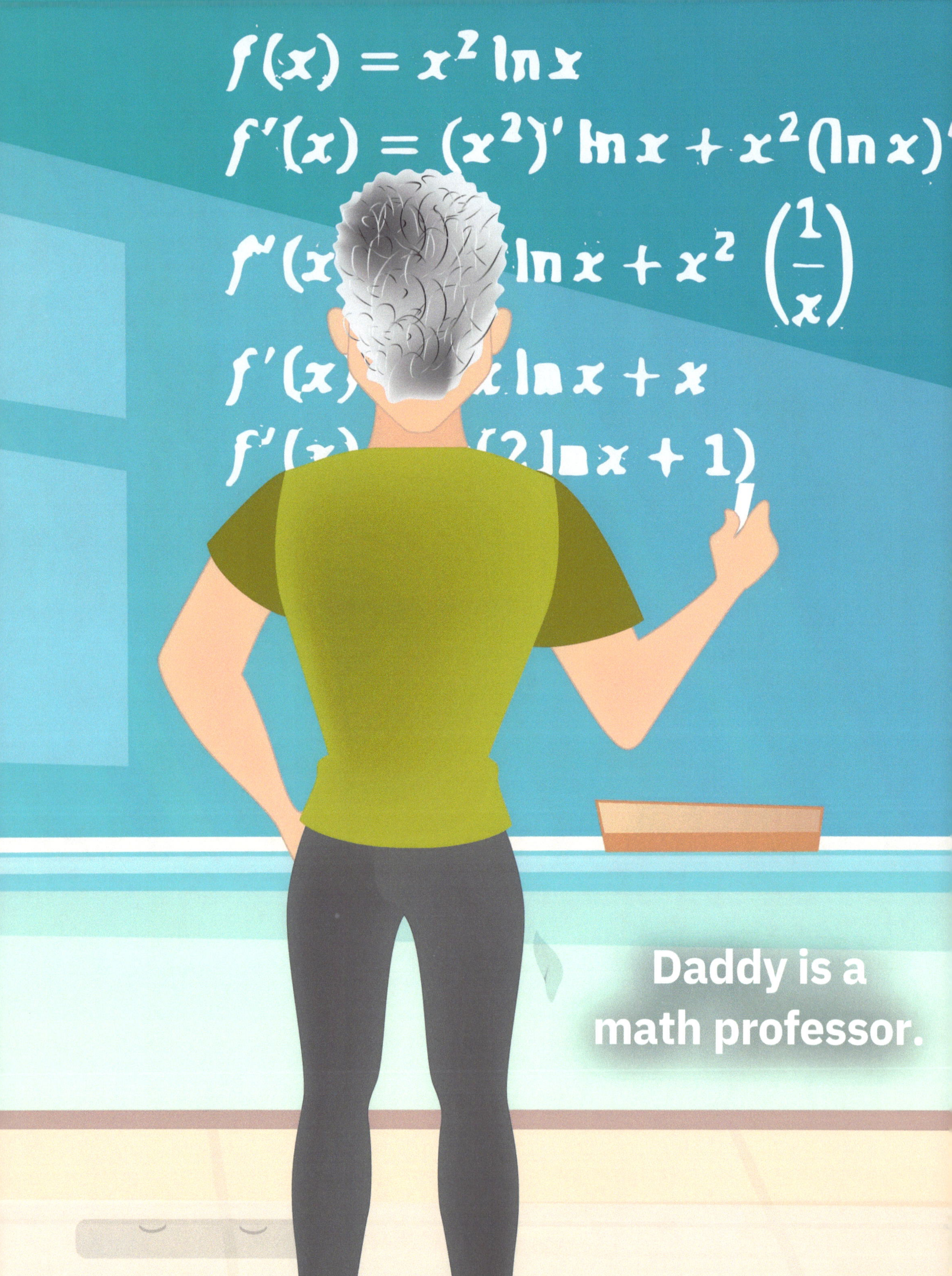

$f(x) = x^2 \ln x$
$f'(x) = (x^2)' \ln x + x^2 (\ln x)'$
$f''(x) \quad \ln x + x^2 \left(\dfrac{1}{x} \right)$
$f'(x) \quad x \ln x + x$
$f'(x) \quad (2 \ln x + 1)$
Daddy is a
math professor.

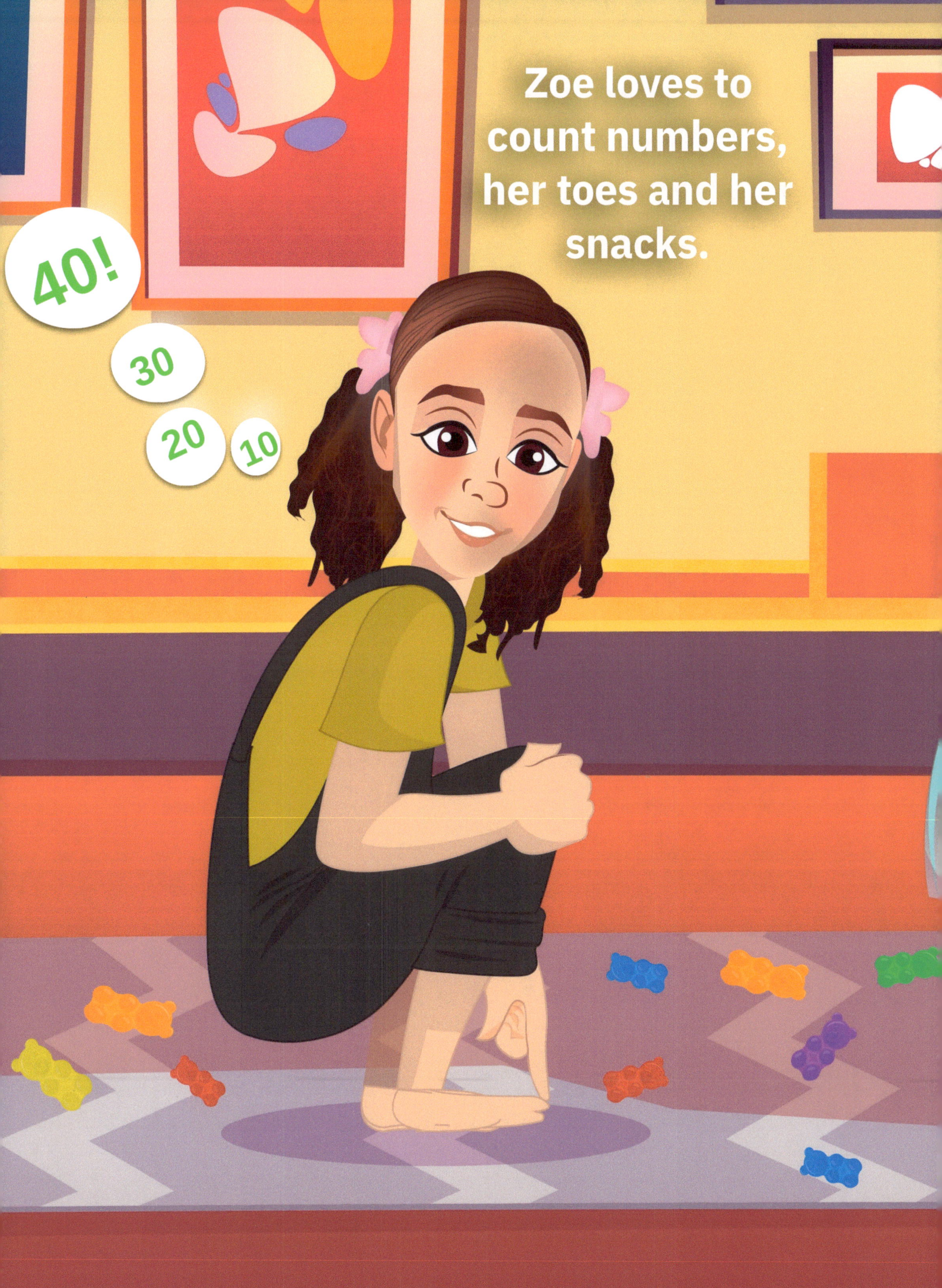
Zoe loves to count numbers, her toes and her snacks.
40!
30
20 10

Zoe and her mommies love to travel, attend play dates and enjoy lots of fun activities. It's extra fun when daddy comes along!

Zoe loves to go outside, and when it rains she sings, "Rain, rain go away!"

One day, Mommy Tiffany and Mommy Yvonne tell Zoe she is going to start something she really loves to do, tomorrow.

"You're going to start swimming lessons!" Mommy Yvonne says.

"There'll be lots of other super 2-year olds learning to swim also and you'll have a teacher named Coach John," adds Mommy Yvonne.

"Bear coming?" asks Zoe.

"No, we don't want bear to get wet, so he'll wait at home for you," says Mommy Tiffany.

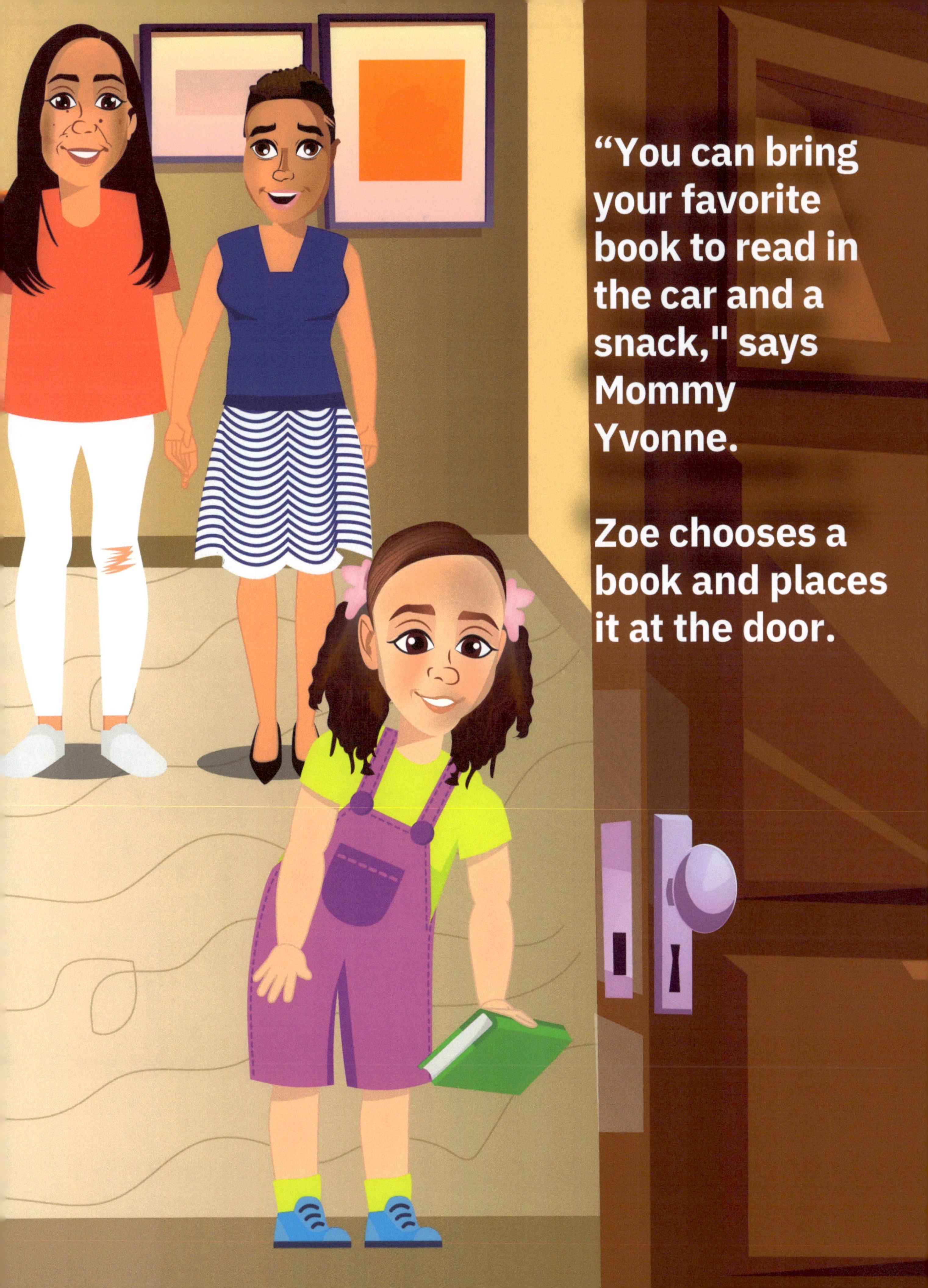

"You can bring your favorite book to read in the car and a snack," says Mommy Yvonne.

Zoe chooses a book and places it at the door.

The morning comes and Zoe is up and ready to go! But first, she washes her face and brushes her teeth. "Water! Pool!" shouts Zoe.

"We're about to leave, but first, someone sent you a video to wish you luck with your swimming lesson today," says Mommy Tiffany.

"Who is it?" says Zoe.

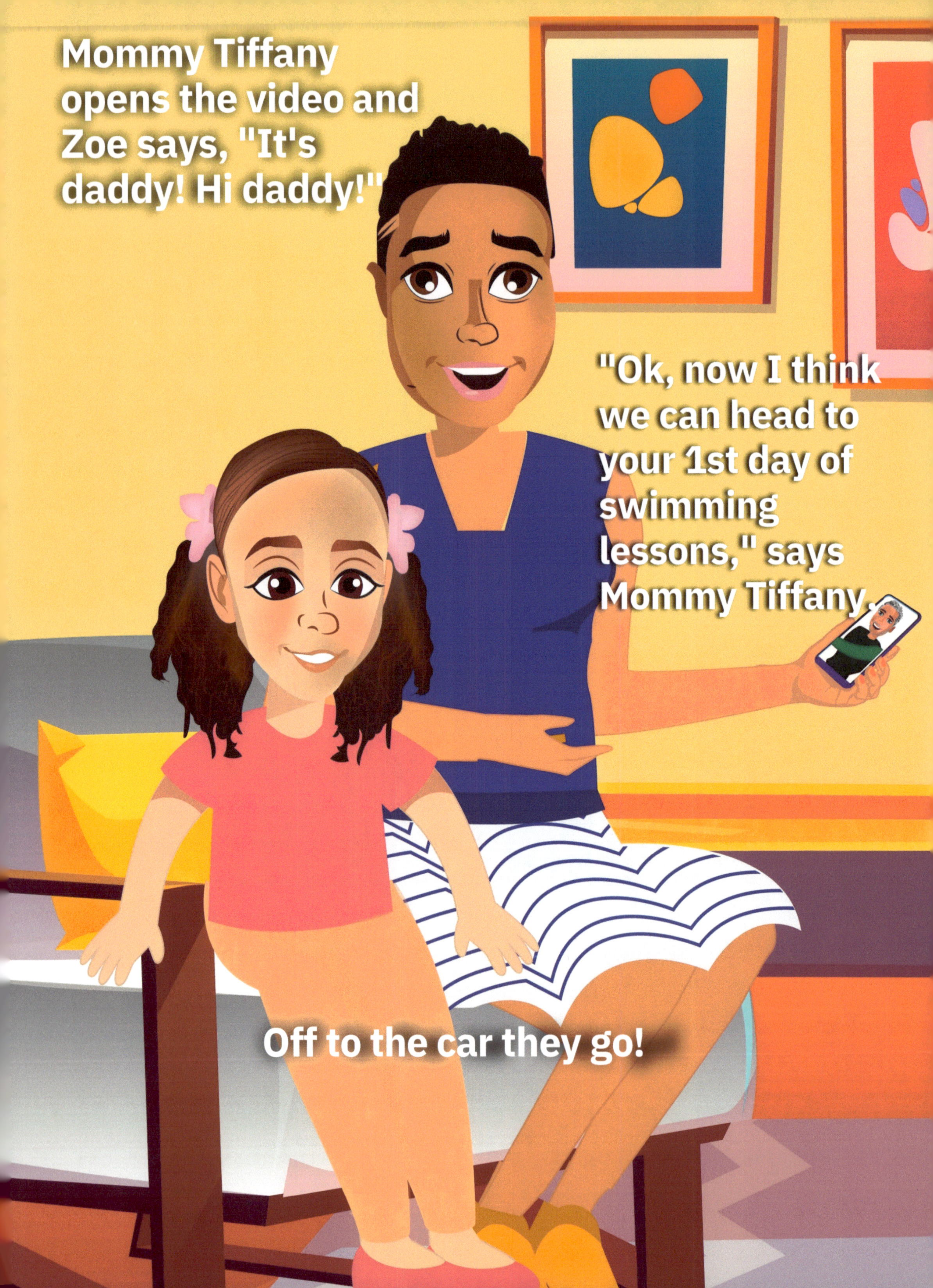

Mommy Tiffany opens the video and Zoe says, "It's daddy! Hi daddy!"
"Ok, now I think we can head to your 1st day of swimming lessons," says Mommy Tiffany.
Off to the car they go!

Zoe is so excited as she walks in with her bathing suit, swim shoes and goggles already on.

"Welcome to swim class Zoe, we're so happy to meet you," says Coach John.

Zoe is a little shy but she happily walks in and is ready to jump into the huge pool!

Mommy Yvonne and Zoe enter the swimming pool with the other four kids, while Mommy Tiffany sits on the bench to take photos.

"First we will start off with free play with your parents," says Coach John.

Lily is already kicking her feet in the water with her mom and dad.

Matt doesn't like the water in his face, so his papa is trying to make it fun.

Lexie won't let her nanny put her down.

Alyssa is trying to float with her aunt.

Cameron decides to
watch on his 1st visit
with his uncle.

Ava is playing catch with her nana.
Seven already knows how to swim, so her babysitter just watches on.

"That's enough for today," says Coach John. "Everyone did great for their first day!

Thank you everyone! It's so special to have family that loves you! It doesn't matter who they are made up of."

"Who loves Zoe?" asks Mommy Tiffany, as they head outside.

"2 Mommies!" shouts Zoe.

"Zoe, look who's waiting by the car!" says Mommy Yvonne.

"Daddy! Daddy! Swimming was fun!" says Zoe.

Mommy Yvonne, Mommy Tiffany, Daddy and Zoe talk all about the first day of swimming as they walk to get ice cream sundaes to celebrate.

THE END.